For my nurslings

Nourishing you has nourished me
in more ways than I could have ever imagined.

All my love always,
Mama

ISBN-10: 0-9971763-1-8
ISBN-13: 978-0-9971763-1-5

My Mama's Milk

Kawani AJ Brown   illustrated by Edward Basil

My Mama's Milk
highlights the mother and child
breastfeeding relationship,
and explores how each mammal
makes milk specifically
for their babies.

Hurry, Mama!

It was sweet and warm and yummy!

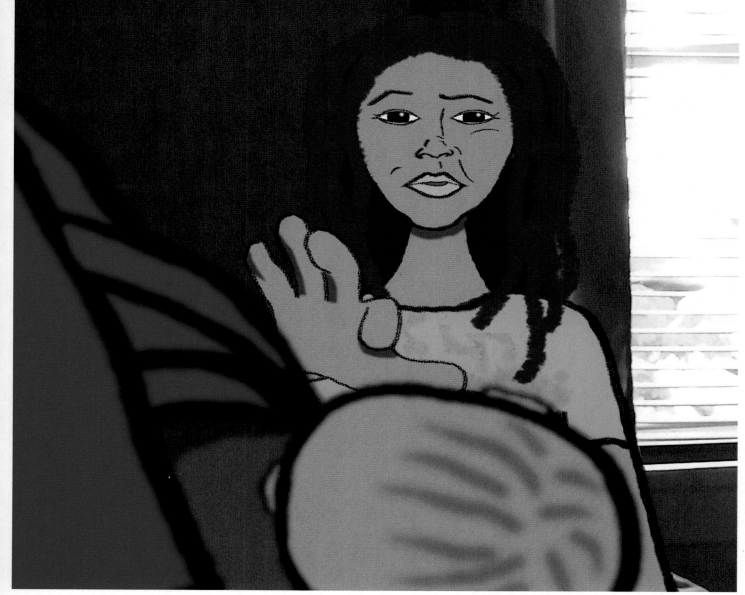

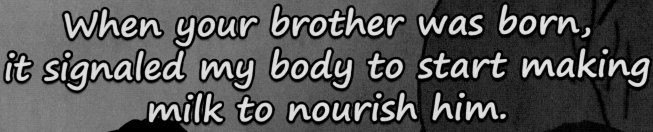

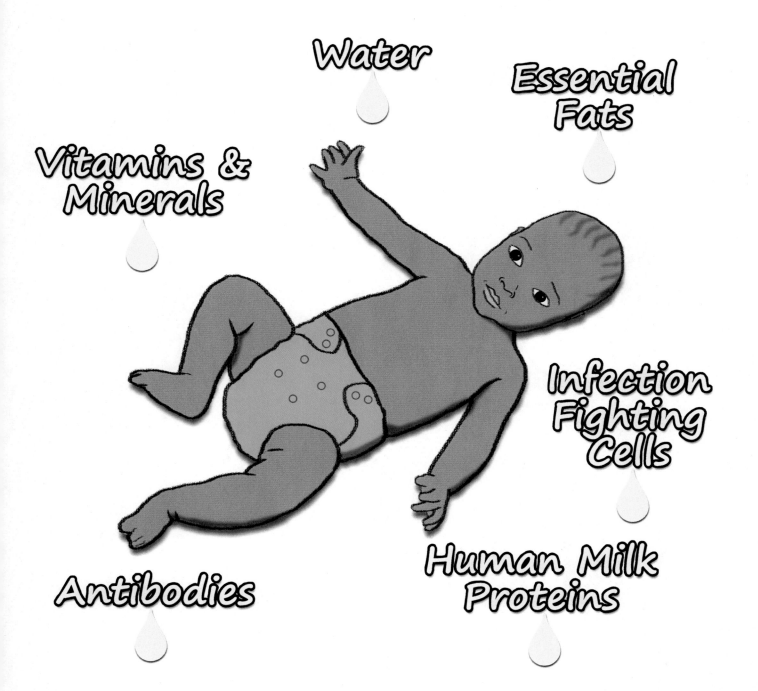

All mammals make milk especially for their babies.

Like mama cows, mama doggies and mama kitties?

Yes, they make milk filled with nutrients just for their little ones,

and my milk is filled with nutrients that were perfect for you and now for your brother.

No not yet,

but they will when you're a Mother.

Made in the USA
Monee, IL
10 December 2022

20702086R00017